Why Airplanes Go Bump in the Clouds

WM. D. BRALEY

Why Airplanes Go Bump in the Clouds

Illustrations By: Dean

PAGE PUBLISHING, INC.
New York, NY

First originally published by Page Publishing, Inc. 2016

ISBN 978-1-68348-279-6 (Paperback)
ISBN 978-1-64027-910-0 (Hardcover)
ISBN 978-1-68348-280-2 (digital)

Printed in the United States of America

Dedication

To my new friend Jaeden Hardison
from Orange City, Iowa

Every morning, it is very busy in heaven. God has to look down on earth at all the people. He sees all the boys, girls, moms, dads, and grandparents.

Then, he has to assign the angels to go down and help the people. Every person on the earth has a special angel assigned to watch over them.

Little Tommy Jones has climbed a tree to get his cat down. Now Tommy and his cat are stuck in the tree. His angel is on the way to watch over him till help can get him down.

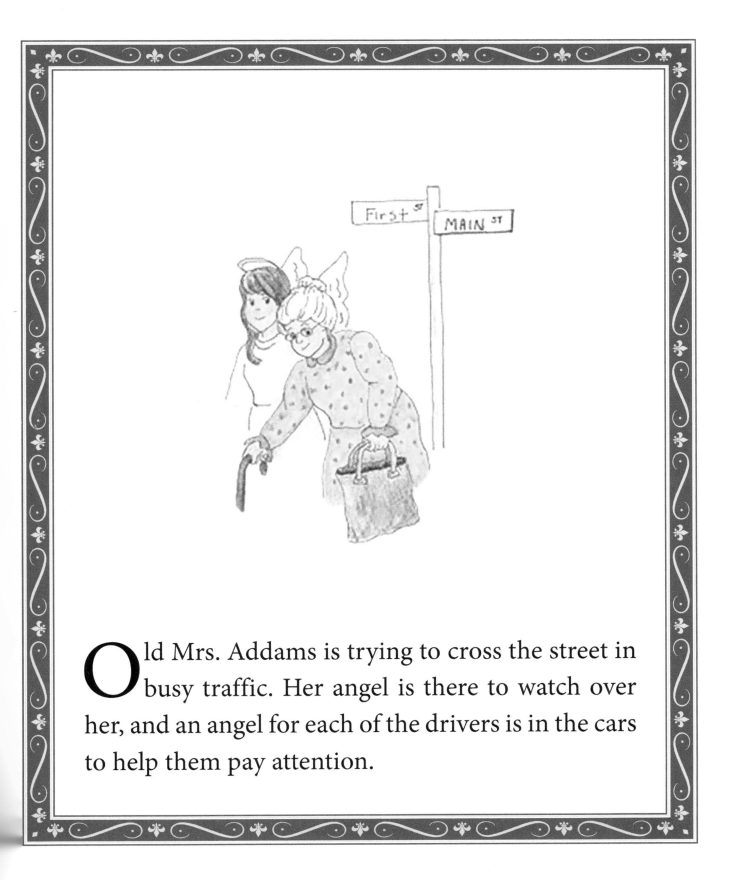

Old Mrs. Addams is trying to cross the street in busy traffic. Her angel is there to watch over her, and an angel for each of the drivers is in the cars to help them pay attention.

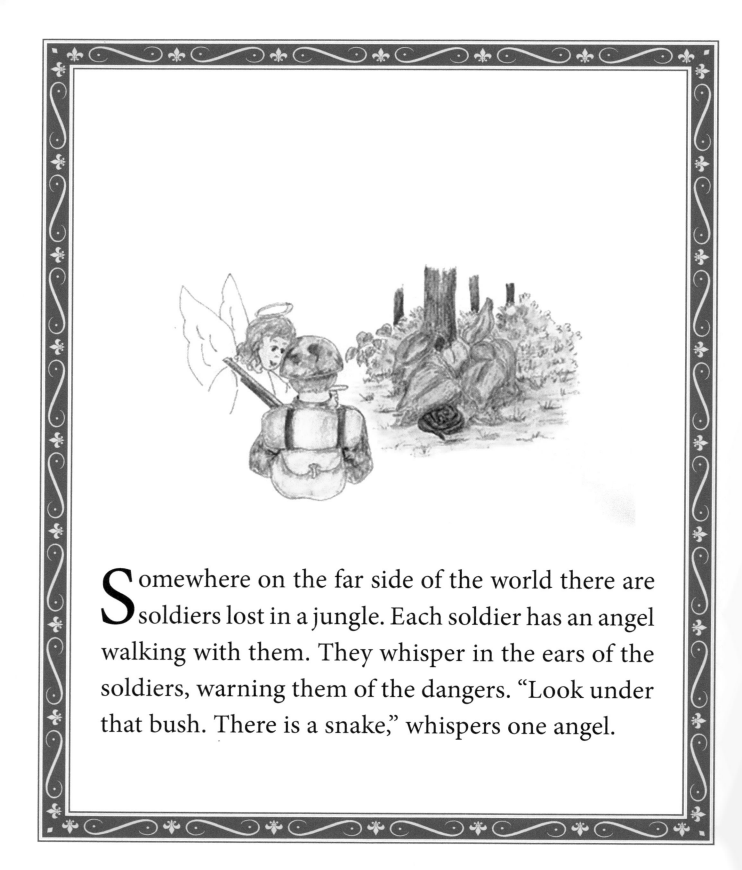

S omewhere on the far side of the world there are soldiers lost in a jungle. Each soldier has an angel walking with them. They whisper in the ears of the soldiers, warning them of the dangers. "Look under that bush. There is a snake," whispers one angel.

Another angel whispers to her soldier, "That trail to the right is the way back to the road." All day long all over the world, the angels are carrying out their assignments.

Now up in heaven every morning, the angels are getting ready for the journey to earth to start their assignments.

The trip down to earth is wonderful with all the white fluffy clouds floating around. The clouds are so beautiful, and they look like giant fluffy pillows. They look so comfortable; the angels sometimes stop to take a break. They laugh and play and bounce around on the fluffy clouds. They start having so much fun, they lose track of time and forget they have people on earth needing their help.

Now, God is always watching from above the clouds. He sees the fun his angels are having, and he loves to see them playing and happy. But he is God, and the people below that he is also watching need their angels.

God is so wise, he does not want to scold the angels, so when an airplane flies by the clouds where the angels are playing, he gently blows his breath on the clouds and sends them floating close to the airplane.

When the plane flies through the clouds, it bounces the angels off and sends them down to take care of the people below. That is why the airplanes sometimes go *bump, bump, bumpity, bump* in the clouds!

So the next time you fly in an airplane and you feel the bumps, don't be afraid.

Look really close into the clouds and you might see the angels playing and bouncing from cloud to cloud.

About the Author

Wm. D. Braley has been writing poetry and short stories since he was thirteen years old. He states that he feels the writings are not his but inspirations from God. He states that he is simply the stenographer. He is a truly inspired author that adds much to each person that reads his poetry and stories. He has a way with allowing God to put his words on paper. Each time someone reads one of his poems or stories, it blesses and inspires them to do better and be a better person. He is a true inspiration to all that know him.